Also by Richard Bach

RICHARD BACH

THE FERRET CHRONICLES

Ferret House Press

THE LAST WAR

Detective Ferrets and the Case of the Golden Deed

SCRIBNER

NEW YORK   LONDON   TORONTO   SYDNEY   SINGAPORE

SCRIBNER
1230 Avenue of the Americas
New York, NY 10020

This book is a work of fiction. Names, characters, places,
and incidents either are products of the author's imagination or
are used fictitiously. Any resemblance to actual events or locales
or persons, living or dead, is entirely coincidental.

First Scribner trade paperback edition 2003

SCRIBNER and design are trademarks of Macmillan Library Reference USA, Inc.,
used under license by Simon & Schuster, the publisher of this work.

For information regarding special discounts for bulk purchases,
please contact Simon & Schuster Special Sales at 1-800-456-6798 or
business@simonandschuster.com

Text set in Fry's Baskerville

Manufactured in the United States of America

1   3   5   7   9   10   8   6   4   2

Library of Congress Cataloging-in-Publication Data

Bach, Richard.
The last war: detective ferrets and the case of the golden deed/Richard Bach.—
1st Scribner trade pbk. ed.
p. cm.—(The ferret chronicles)
1. Ferrets—Fiction. I. Title.

PS3552.A255L37 2003
813'.54—dc21
2003053944

ISBN 0-7432-2756-5

FOREWORD

I traveled the kingdom of Oz when I was a kid, every book, and there were fourteen of them. In love with the characters, in love with the enchanted land of their adventures.

"Is it real, Mom? Is Oz real?"

She replied as mothers get to do, sometimes, one sentence that lasts a lifetime: "It's real in the writer's mind, Richard, and now it's real in yours."

That was the first day I met good-news bad-news: Oz exists! (You can't get there by train.)

As I didn't know just then how to ask what was on my mind, I spent the next half century framing my questions:

> If Oz exists in our mind, then can no one destroy it, ever?
> Is the world in our mind, too, and not outside?
> What if all we see about us are reflections of what we think is so?
> What's reflected when we decide to change our thought?

Thanks to those early journeys deep into lands beyond maps, here I stand today, bored at last to stone with dramas about evil, films about war and malice and crime. I promised that if I had to watch one more prison scene, one more aggression, one more gigantic spectacular stupendous explosion on-screen, fiction or non, I'd walk out and rebuild the universe.

—Boom—

What if something happened, I got to wondering as I walked away, and a culture grew up without evil, without crime or war? What would it do with all the energies that we squander on our destructions?

How would it feel to live in a world where we choose our highest right and not our darkest wrong, where we lift each other instead of always and ever putting each other down?

How could such a civilization begin, and where would it go?

So were born *The Ferret Chronicles,* the story of a doomed civilization that returned to life upon the single act of one individual.

—Richard Bach

The Ferrets and the Humans

Once there was a team of ferrets, exploring mysteries, who landed upon a small blue planet and discovered a hidden valley that opened onto the land of the humans. The ferrets found these creatures a promising species, of grace and charm, intelligence and curiosity, of warm humor and great courage.

Because of this, and because of the dangers and promises ahead for the young race, the ferrets gave to the humans four powers with which they could prevail over the challenges to come.

The first was the power of fire, the second was the power of the wheel, the third was the power of written language, the fourth was the power of courtesy and respect, one to another.

The humans were quick to learn, and cherished the gifts that the ferrets had brought. As the explorers prepared to depart, the humans begged them to stay and to share with humankind the delight of the brave new civilization that would rise.

The ferrets were touched, and promised to return. On the day of their departure, one human turned to them. "Of these powers, dear ferrets, which is the first among them, which would you have us guard above all others?"

"Well asked," replied the ferrets. "Without fire can you prosper, and without the wheel, and without the alphabet, for many have prospered on your planet and across the galaxies without these. The one power without which no civilization can long survive, however, is the last, the power of courtesy and respect for each other and for all life."

The humans murmured, understanding, and used their new letters to scribe the Courtesies on tablets of onyx, the words finished in purest silver. When the ferrets had departed, the new race learned swiftly, mastering the natures of fire and wheel and alphabet.

They pondered long, however, how best to protect the most precious of powers, and at last it was agreed to keep the Tablets of the Courtesies in the safest place their world could offer. From reverence, no copy was made, nor were its holy words read but by those who first had heard them from the ferrets.

And so it came to pass that the one essential of the Four Gifts was weighted in rare metals and precious jewels, locked within a giant chest of iron, and after a long voyage and with great ceremony, was given to *the waves and buried, safe forever in the uttermost part of the sea.*

How others deal with gifts we've given is not our decision, but theirs.

— Antonius Ferret, *Fables*

THE LAST WAR

Detective Ferrets and the Case of the Golden Deed

CHAPTER 1

Shamrock Ferret set a cup of Mandalay blackberry tea on the side table, tilted a tiny pitcher to add a dash of honey (poured, not stirred) and curled herself in the comfort of her Cases Unsolved chair. The antique she had bought at a used-thing sale, whirl-dots for pattern, soft as woven sunlight.

As the fire warmed the hearth and her own sable-chocolate fur, the detective set a small disk of black felt upon the chair and reviewed the facts.

The patterns of cornstalks fallen in the fields were always finished and complete; they were ever the same, almost an insignia: two stars, one large, one small, joined by a sweeping curved pathway.

The patterns had always been discovered in the morning, having appeared sometime between dusk and dawn, under a full moon. There were no marks of tools or machinery of any kind. There was no reason for the designs, nor meaning in them.

Here she reached a paw to stroke her whiskers as she stared into the light of the fire, and corrected herself.

No apparent reason, she thought. Every mystery cloaks an inner reason, each one gives its meaning only when we have allowed ourselves a new point of view. There are no secrets, she had learned. Through observation, inquiry, through the kaleidoscope of intuition, we detect what has been facing us all along.

She sipped her tea in the office of her flat, watching the fire.

About her in the modest dark-paneled room stood her desk with notepads and pens, the old clock which had ticked in her home since she was a kit, her microscope, brass polished, focus knob worn from use. Here were her shelves of books: *Analysis* from *Zero, Principles of Deduction* and thirty volumes of *The Paws of Knowledge,* a set much lined and dog-eared. From a peg on the wall hung her crimson tam-o'-shanter and snow-color scarf of many pockets. By the door a letter-drop and a whimsical bell made from an old ship's telegraph, the pointer at *Engines Standby.* All peaceful stillness.

Within her was no such quiet. She watched the fire, yet behind her eyes flashed scene after instant scene—the patterns, the clues, connections between the known and the possible.

Miss Shamrock Ferret earned her living by imagining possibilities, and now the images tumbled like a runaway slide show. Scene after scene rose and fell, possibilities slanting at the wrong angle, near misses, pictures out of match with the portrait of a mystery.

Now she lifted the disk of felt, and holding it gently between her paws, she closed her eyes, opened a door of imagination.

How I love this job, she thought, breathing the scent of Mandalay. How I love *finding out!*

CHAPTER 2

It was dark at the top of the mountain, and that is why they had come, nine kits and Miss Ginger Ferret, all warm scarves and hats, journeyed here to settle on moss and grass, tails curled about them, eyes wide in starlight.

"Turning way out in space," said their teacher, "there are millions of stars around us. And in all the sky, one of them is your own. You'll know your star when you see it. It will be the warmest, the most friendly of all, and when it whispers to you, reach up your paw and say hello."

A little voice in the night: "My own star, Miss Ginger?"

"Your very own. Always you'll remember this night. Even when tonight has drifted into long ago, when many things have changed, when you're flying free and when you're deep in tests and challenge, your star will be with you still. Your star."

Fluffy masks and whiskers turned upward, scanned from horizon to zenith.

"Which is *your* star, Miss Ginger?"

The teacher pointed southward. "See the Seven Kits, Jimkin, four in a straight line with the triangle on top? Mine is Corrista, the second brightest, sparkling blue."

Ginger remembered the night she had first seen her star, shining silent above the meadow not far from her home. How constant had it been, and how reassuring, that light in the sky! Since that hour, Corrista had twinkled as though it knew everything was going to turn out for the best, no matter whether Ginger cried sometimes, or doubted her destiny. And ever had her star been right.

One voice after another, the teacher heard from the young ferrets, saw paws reaching. "Hello . . ."

Ginger Ferret knelt by them each, looking into the heavens. "The blue one there, Mikela, is that your star?"

"Yes, Miss Ginger."

"It's called Veya, in the constellation of Erinaceus, the Hedgehog. See his nose, and his ears? So Veya is his eye. The story goes that the hedgehog once saved the life of a baby meadow vole in the night, when it slipped and fell into a stream above the rapids. Erinaceus splashed into the water, lifted out the baby, returned it to its parents' burrow and went upon his way, thinking nothing of it. But Mustella, the Great Ferret, was watching from above and saw what had happened. So it came to pass that at the end of his life on Earth, the hedgehog was lifted up into the stars, for all to see and remember to be kind to the smallest living thing."

While the galaxy wheeled slow motion overhead, Ginger Ferret told the kits the names of the stars they had chosen. With her paw she outlined their constellations, told the stories of how each had come to be in the sky. She told them the legend that ferrets themselves had left their home planet a hundred centuries ago and come to Earth from another sun and a different planet.

She showed them the Polecat star, around which all the others turned, and the twinkling outline of Mustella herself nearby, body shaped like a water dipper, its handle become the Great Ferret's tail, four bright stars curving down and up again.

"The legend says that Mustella is the only constellation in the sky that looks the same from Earth as it does from Ferra."

"Is that true, Miss Ginger, or is that a story like Erinaceus?"

"Most stories grow from what's true. Hedgehogs are kind to meadow voles, even today. But no one's quite sure where we come from."

The last of the kits waited patiently, listening, watching the others.

"Have you found your star, Shamrock?" asked her teacher.

The little one pointed. "Yes, ma'am. It's there, in the Great Ferret."

"The edge of the dipper, the brightest one?"

"No. In the middle of it."

A shock of heat went through the teacher, from her nose to her tail. Could this kit have chosen . . .

"Draw two lines, corner to corner, in the square. Right near where they come together. It's not very bright."

The teacher turned to the little ferret. "Of all the stars in the sky," she murmured, "that's who called to you, the one at Mustella's heart?"

"Yes, ma'am . . . is that all right? It's not very big . . ."

"Do you know the name of that star?"

"No, ma'am."

"Shamrock, that's Pherrine. The legend says that's the star of our home planet."

"Why is it a story, Miss Ginger? Why don't we *know*?"

The teacher smiled, wistful in the dark, some deep spark of her soul yearning for home. "What are you most curious about, Shamrock? Things that have already happened, or things that are going to happen?"

A silence while the little one thought it through. Her mother and father had asked her questions all her life, showed her how to observe, to imagine, to research, deduce: "Why is it so, Shamrock? Why did this happen as it did, and not some other way, or not at all?"

"I'm most curious about . . . *anything that's a mystery!*"

This one could widen the world, her teacher thought.

A white-masked kit stood near, listening. "*I'm* most curious about what's going to happen!"

The teacher nodded. "You're like most of us, Hopper. What's already happened, our own history, isn't as exciting for us as creating new futures." She smiled. "Why not, Shamrock?"

"Because we can make any future come true," said the kit, "because the future isn't finished. The past is."

A voice in the dark: Jimkin. "But can't we change the past, too, Miss Ginger, if we really want to?"

"Philosopher ferrets say we can."

"I want to be a philosopher ferret," said Jimkin.

Whether such would be the path for one of her kits their teacher couldn't say. Every ferret is a magical creature, she knew, and now the night had split, skyrockets into nine new tomorrows. In each of the nine lived a kit with its own star to be a friend, for always and ever.

CHAPTER 3

By the time Shamrock arrived, the meeting hall of the village was filled with farmer ferrets. She had promised a solution to the mystery in their cornfields and no one wanted to be last to hear.

The hall went quiet as she walked to a stage framed in the inks of drying maize and the pastels of this season's pumpkins and squash. Centerstage stood a table lit by an overhead light.

She set a wicker cake-basket upon the table, unsnapped four brass latches but did not remove the cover, left it there under the light. Whispers through the crowd: What's in the box?

She lifted a paw-held microphone and the whispers subsided. "Thank you, gentleferrets," she began, the clear, firm voice of a skilled investigator. "The Case of the Curious Patterns has been a wonderful challenge for us all." She paused, looking from face to face, a room of many-shaded furs and masks, of eyes watching as though she were the illusionist come to explain a magic.

"Help me test my answer," she said, "with some questions for you."

At once her listeners changed from observers to players in a game of wits with the unknown. *Help me test my answer* was to become quintessential Shamrock Ferret, her clients enlisted to become detectives themselves.

"Concerning the fields where the patterns have appeared," she asked, "has there always been a stream, larger than a brook but smaller than a river, within a thousand paws' distance?"

A murmur through the hall, a nodding of whiskers and masks, a chorus of assent. Yes, as a matter of

fact, every field with a crop pattern did lie not far distant from a stream neither large nor small.

"Have the fields, as one faces north, always been to the left of the river, and never to the right?"

Thoughtful nods. Yes, that is so.

"Has a pattern ever appeared after a foggy or rainy night, or has the sky been clear, before a pattern is found?"

Silence of her clients reflecting upon the matter, then nodding, confirming with each other, and once again the voice of assent. The weather had been fine, every night a pattern was formed.

Shamrock nodded her thanks for their help. "Has this last season been an unusually prosperous one? Would anyone say that this has been a difficult year for farming?"

A sparkle of laughter through the crowd. By no means had this been a hard year for agriculture. Though they worked from dawn to dusk through the whole land of trim farms and tended fields nearby, the ferrets and their village had prospered.

"Does anyone recognize this?" She held up the disk of felt, the shape of a beret, half the size of her paw.

A word from the fourth row, surprise and shock. "Why, I found one of those! On my hilltop field, in the April pattern!"

"So there you have it," said Shamrock. "Thank you, gentleferrets, the case has been a wonderful challenge. I appreciate the honor of your invitation to solve it. Your mystery designs, your crop patterns, are the work of *visiting Parisian artist mice.*"

Silence from the group, paws moving to stroke whiskers as they watched Shamrock.

If the detective had a favorite moment in the solution of a case, it was this one, laying the answer before her clients, watching disbelief melt in the heat of evidence.

"When the iron molecules within it have been magnetized," she explained, "a cornstalk will bend swiftly and permanently upon the application of only one substance: painters' flax-leaf oil. The artists prefer to work near the left bank of a stream, as they are accustomed to, of course, in Paris. Clear skies are required, and the light of a full moon, to inspire the lunatic in creative minds which would not otherwise consider such a lark. Of course, as would be expected in any large group of travelers, someone loses their hat."

"Why do they need our fields, Miss Shamrock, and cornstalks for their canvas? If the design comes to them in the full moon, why don't they . . . paint it at home?"

The detective nodded. "That's a good question. The designs do not come to the artists, though, the artists come to the designs. Your corn *is* their canvas. Your fine deep soil was altered many centuries ago, the iron oxide polarized by intense magnetic fields.

"The mice don't create the figures, but they sense where they are, and with their oil they free the cornstalks to flow the way paint flows, following electric brushstrokes long past."

A different voice from the audience. "How can the mice know to do this, Miss Shamrock, when it's never occurred to us that we have patterns in the ground?"

"These are artist mice," said the detective, "sensitive to the currents of worlds the rest of us do not feel. Butterflies migrate around the earth for reasons they do not know, and in the same way these delicate creatures have been led to your fields, sensing only that art lies beneath."

"Then there must be other patterns, waiting!"

"Most likely, yes."

"But Miss Shamrock, what do the patterns mean?"

Here the young detective frowned. "You've asked me to solve the mystery of the crop pattern appearances," she replied, "how was the corn bent, who entered your fields, and why. What the patterns mean is a different mystery, one I haven't solved. Off the tip of my tail, a guess before evidence, I'd suspect the patterns are a message left here by the ancients, to remind us of something important."

"Remind us?"

"What do philosopher ferrets say? *We know all there is to know. There's nothing learned, but remembered.*"

Came a voice from the center of the meeting. "Have you other proof of your Parisian artist-mouse hypothesis? You've said the left bank, but how are you certain they were Parisian mice? It may sound a little far-fetched to others . . ."

It was still fresh in her mind, her vision, holding the miniature beret. Closing her eyes was like opening them in a different place, the home of the French cap and its owner, in the studio of the artist mice.

"We invent nothing," their leader had exclaimed to the artists, their brushes and flax-leaf oil packed into battered valises. *"We discover! We liberate the art within!"*

In her mind she had traveled with them to the fields beyond the sleeping ferret village, had watched the mice brush the oils deftly, seen the cornstalks collapse under moonlight to follow the curving energies of forces laid down long ago.

But to others a different answer could still be true. So much to explain!

"Of course," she said. "How *are* we certain they are Parisian mice? If you wish to explore the left banks of the streams near any crop pattern, you will find underground entrances to the staging areas for the artists. When you do, you will find the pawprints of many individuals, and you may find something like this, as well . . ."

She held up a scrap of colored paper and read, *"Chemin de fer de Paris à Londres, tout ensemble."*

She spoke to the last row in the hall. "This, gentle-ferrets, is a group-excursion railway ticket, purchased for the evening train, on the date of the appearance of our latest pattern."

"A coincidence?" someone asked. "Can we be certain?"

"What do the patterns have to do with our prosperity?" asked another. "Why did you need to know if this has been a good year for us?"

"Allow me to answer both questions at once," said Shamrock. "A coincidence? And, what does your prosperity have to do with the mystery?"

She tapped briskly on the cover of the wicker cake-basket centerstage, then lifted it and set it aside.

Blinking under the light and rising from a tiny lounge chair by a table set with fresh-baked bread and chunks of Camembert, stood a European field-mouse, brown-whiskered, dressed in a grand bow tie of flowing silks, a black felt beret to match the one the detective had displayed earlier.

Shamrock extended the microphone toward the creature.

"Bonjour, mes amis," said the diminutive artist, his voice amplified in the speakers. "This is a good question, your prosperity."

The audience gasped. It would have been enough for Shamrock to have explained the mystery. She was not required to produce the principals.

"We are, how do you say . . . *la lune* . . . we are lunatic on certain evenings, when the moon is full. We are not malicious." After the astonishment, not a sound from the audience, staring from the mouse to Shamrock and back again.

The rodent looked to the detective, then back to the farmer ferrets. "We would not have appeared," he said, "nor have done our work, if to bend the corn would have brought you not wonder but hardship."

Then it was silent. Hearing no further questions, the little animal reached a paw toward the cheese, lifted a morsel.

"Hurray for the mice!" cried one of the farmers. "Shall we invite them to visit now as our guests, by first-class railway, to bring their paintings and show them in the square?"

The mouse set down its meal and swept the cap from its head in a flourishing bow to all, its nose nearly touching the floor of the case.

So ended the meeting in a round of cheers for the artists, and a cheer for Shamrock, too, along with payment for contract complete and mystery solved.

On the way home, the ferret train chuffing from the dark of a tunnel into daylight, Shamrock made a note from her own unquenched curiosity: *What do the patterns mean?*

CHAPTER 4

Burrows Ferret returned to the city not long after Shamrock, immersed the whole drive in thought, fascinated with the detective's solution to the Case of the Curious Patterns.

He watched the highway curl and divide past the windscreen of his Austin-Furet, glanced at a road sign:

Please maintain
the speed

at which you feel safe
under these conditions

He touched the tape recorder in his scarf pocket.

"Not only has our young detective solved the mystery," he said, "but as with the Case of the Flying Delphin and the Case of the Too Many Blossoms, she did it in a few hours, a morning's investigation and an evening's analysis at most.

"Her tests must continue, of course, but it seems that we have a powerful candidate on our paws.

"Advise N and S," he said.

An afterthought: ". . . and ZZ."

He turned off the recorder. What would our civilization be, he thought, if we had no examples?

CHAPTER 5

From the day she was born, Shamrock Ferret was surrounded in questions.

"Look at the bubbles, Shamrock!" her mother would say, bathing her kit. "Why are they round instead of square? Why don't they sink in the water?

"Why does the sky change colors, little Shamrock? Where do stars go in the daytime? What do clouds weigh?"

"Hallo, Shamrock," her father would say, morning-times. "Are you sure we're awake, and not dreaming breakfast? Why do we dream at all?"

Her parents ever were asking why, and little Shamrock loved to answer, making up explanations when she didn't know. Questions were feather-touch tensions, answers made the tensions go, left a warm place where they had been.

Psychometry, at first, was a game. "This scarf was worn by a very special ferret," her parents said. "Hold it in your paws, close your eyes, tell us what it was like to be this animal." And sure enough, there were visions in the dark, beginnings of a skill that would help their kit no matter which direction her curiosity might lead.

"Can you hold the box," they asked, "and tell us where it came from?

"Trust your imagination, Shamrock. If it feels like you're inventing a story, invent away! The stories you imagine are probably true."

Instead of leaving her powers behind as she grew, the kit developed them; practice made her what others called a *sensitive*. No one discouraged or ridiculed her interests, in the ferret way they encouraged them instead, delighting in her adventures as she did in others'.

Shamrock grew to excel not only in psychometry, but in logic, in analysis, deduction, cryptography, patterns. Grown-ups coming to visit would bring thousand-piece puzzles, watch while the kit assembled them in minutes, humming tunes to herself. They'd shake their heads and smile, bewildered. If it was a test of mind, Shamrock Ferret could solve it, often in several ways.

She painted one bedroom wall herself, from a photo of the famous storefront office: *Nutmeg & Bergamont,* an arc of gold letters on black glass, *Detectives,* a mirrored arc beneath.

In the research drawer of her little desk were news clippings of Nutmeg Ferret's cases, Shamrock's notes on how the celebrated investigator had solved them, step by step, how she might have solved them differently.

Nutmeg's Case of the Missing Star, of the Tilted Factory, of the Secret Gift, every clue explained in a whirl of sparkling insight at the end, as breathtaking to the kit as were high-wire acrobatics to others.

Investigating her heroine, Shamrock found that Nutmeg Ferret had been a kit from a northcountry village, fur like smooth cinnamon, modest and soft-spoken. Her gift was to take the complicated apart, piece by piece, with questions so simple that they answered themselves.

"Now, why would this be?" In time, the power of her words had made it a household phrase to ferrets around the world. Puzzled, they'd echo the sleuth of the spice-color fur: *Now, why would this be?*

There's a reason I can't get enough of Nutmeg, wrote Shamrock to her diary: *The Case of My Favorite Detective.* It's that level, open gaze. Every magazine photo, television interview, I can see it. Nutmeg Ferret misses nothing. As soon as she notices, she understands. When I think of her, everything in the world makes sense.

Nutmeg's life is all purpose and adventure, thought Shamrock, and as though she were already the detective she yearned to be, the kit was happiest wondering, investigating, bringing the hidden to light. Alone in her room, she whispered, "I'll be like Nutmeg, someday."

Not long after, a strange thing—a salesferret had called: large, light-masked and a little unkempt, as though his fur had been brushed backward here and there, a bundle of brochures and a volume from *The Paws of Knowledge.*

He thanked her parents for their time, accepted a place on the sofa. "A world of research on one shelf!" he told them. "Everything your kit will want to know. Not quite, with a mind like hers, but she'll find

Most Everything About Most Everything, as we like to say. With *The Paws of Knowledge,* why, there'll be no mystery she can't solve!"

At this her mum and dad had looked keenly at the salesferret. Chance turn of phrase, or had the big animal guessed their kit's passion for the unknown?

He handed his sample (*Volume 13: Megalith to Nudibranch*) to the youngster studying him. "Open it anywhere, Miss Shamrock."

As luck would have it, the page fell open to *Mysteries, Great, of the World.* Halfway down the text an outline began:

> *Aircraft, Unknown:*
> *Alphabet, Ancient Ferrune:*
> *Aqua-Bees:*

Found only in Loch Stoat, near the palace at Mustelania, aqua-bees are said to nest underwater, rising to the surface and flying to pollinate undetermined flowers in or near the palace before returning. No study has been devised to learn the secrets of the aqua-bee without disturbing its home or habits, so little is known of these rare creatures. Local legend, however . . .

Little is known . . . no phrase could be more magnetic to Shamrock Ferret.

She clasped the volume to her, the book nearly half her height. "Oh, *please!*" she implored. "Mum, Dad, there's so much to learn! Did you know, at the palace there are *aqua-bees?*"

Her parents looked at each other, then to the sales-ferret. *The Paws of Knowledge* was thirty volumes of higher education, an investment far beyond the budget of their little household.

After their visitor had left, the kit's parents reminded, "You have the museum, not far away, you have the library . . ."

"But I can't jump from one to . . . Dad, I can't check out *thirty volumes!*"

"Can't," said her father. "There's a strong word, Shamrock . . ."

She apologized, and found that she could check out three volumes at a time, of the ten-volume kit's edition of *Paws,* simple words and pictures.

She did not ask her parents how it was that the salesferret had known her name, why he had rubbed chalk to lighten his mask, nor did she tell them later that her investigation showed he had visited no other house on her block and, as far as she could tell, no other in her neighborhood.

What would Nutmeg Ferret have to say about this? Nutmeg would begin at the beginning, she thought: *Now, why would this be?* Yet for once the question did not resolve itself for Shamrock, the kit unwilling to see the simple answer.

Late one afternoon, carrying volumes Four through Six home from the library, she saw from afar that a heavy wooden crate had been left upon her doorstep. Her parents did not leave packages untended on the step, so the kit knew that whoever had left it had not rung the doorbell.

Why would this be? Because they did not wish to be identified.

She ran the rest of the way home.

The crate had no return address, no delivery markings, though her scarf-pocket magnifying glass hinted that it had been wheeled there from a closed vehicle on a red paw-trolley. Two words, *Shamrock Ferret,* had been stenciled in black ink on the wood.

The screen door opened as she finished her search for clues. "Hallo," said her father, "what do we have here?"

He opened the crate for her, but his kit already knew. It was the adult edition, all thirty volumes: *The Paws of Knowledge.*

⌢
‥

Neither family nor friends were surprised when it happened that Shamrock's pastime became her profession, when the young ferret opened an office at last, a small room in her flat at 7 Blessingthorpe Lane, near the edge of the city: *Shamrock Ferret, Detective.*

Looking back, her neighbors told the press that they had always known it would happen. The kit was the sweetest little thing, thoughtful, kind to everyone. Never had her family been rich, but my, that youngster was brilliant, always had a way of solving puzzles.

What her neighbors didn't know was that long before she had cracked the Case of the Curious Patterns, before she had solved the Case of the Flying Delphin, even before she had opened her office, Shamrock Ferret was being watched.

CHAPTER 6

The Museum of Ancient Times had ever been a magnet for Shamrock. Old things fascinated, early tools and housewares and instruments in the Hall of Artifacts, boats and carriages in the Hall of Travel. Now the pattern in the cornfields was a constant engine within, driving her with its mystery—something old had caused those designs.

Today she entered the Hall of Paintings, just completed, high windows over sheer marble walls.

Lost in thought, she walked with a crowd of visitors between scenes ordered by centuries. Here a ferret merchant ship, flags before the wind, bright sails on a sea of double-sky blue, laden with silks and spices. So fine the art that one could distinguish the masks and whiskers of the animals in the rigging, the helmsferret at the wheel.

Down the way, a work found in the catacombs of the Lost City, thought to be of Pheretima herself, at the palace.

The patterns were laid down centuries ago, thought Shamrock. To solve the puzzle of their meaning, do I have to solve the puzzle of our own origins, as well?

At the end of the hallway, a simple canvas. It showed a silvery blue vase of pale blossoms, set on the sill of an oval window overlooking a tapestry of polka dots.

Oldest Known Ferret Painting, said a plaque beneath the wooden frame. *Subject: Flowers.*

Shamrock slowed, stopped there, the crowd parting, flowing around her. How could art from long ago be so familiar? The flowers, painted in exquisite detail, were common enough, *Dodecatheon furetii,* the delicate Shooting Star of the parks and fields.

The detective stared at the painting. Somewhere she had seen this vase. Where?

Her powers of recall, often extraordinary, offered random guesses. In the show windows of Furry Home, they suggested. No. In a curio shop as you passed. The shop was . . . where? It was . . . don't tell us . . . it was . . . there are so many shop windows . . .

While she waited for her answer, Shamrock studied the painting, tilted her head to see the vase from a different angle.

At last the recall division of her mind reached its limits. We're sorry, we don't know where you saw it. Patience, please. It will come to us.

Shamrock sighed, shook her head. She left the museum and headed home, haunted by the feeling that she had been remembering her future, that the painting had a value to her that she could not place.

Had it been a coincidence, she chanced upon the old scene, this day, this hour, this moment? She shook her head. What had happened was no coincidence—coincidence is always an answer to questions we have asked.

What do the patterns mean?

When she opened her door, a card fell from the handle to the threshold. She stooped to retrieve it and read:

Burrows Ferret
Nutmeg & Bergamont, Detectives

CHAPTER 7

"Would you care for tea, Miss Shamrock?"

"Please don't bother, Mr. Burrows."

"No bother, ma'am. I have it here." Burrows Ferret set the tea service upon her desk, poured a cup of Mandalay blackberry for the detective. From a pitcher of honey, a small dollop. Sprig of mint, twist of lime.

"Here you are, ma'am."

"Thank you!" Shamrock felt as if she should be the one serving tea to her new associate.

Sometimes butler, sometimes sleuth, Burrows had left his card not so long ago, yet at once had he become indispensable.

A large, dark-masked creature, fur the color of mahogany, he had a remarkable mind for detail, Shamrock found, a talent for deduction and rather considerable experience at detecting, having been employed at Nutmeg & Bergamont for quite some time before starting a brief practice on his own.

"I found that I don't work as well alone as I do with others, Miss Shamrock," he had said after she had read his understated résumé. "I've been following your cases and frankly am quite impressed with your skills. If you would do me the honor of testing me in your office, I suspect that you might find yourself considerably less burdened by detail."

Shamrock had watched him closely. Modest to the point of self-effacing, there was something about Burrows vaguely familiar, as determined and constant as a star above.

"Small cases are my specialty," he had told her. "The greater mysteries seem to be yours, if you will forgive my observation. I enjoy discussion and analysis. I have learned how to ask a question. It could be that we might make an excellent team."

So had Shamrock been impressed, these last weeks, so had she enjoyed his mind and manner, that today she asked a question of her own. Picking a card from her desktop, she offered it for his inspection. "Look at this, would you please, Mr. Burrows? Tell me what you think."

He studied it, turned it over. It was what it appeared to be, a business card. Yet the lettering startled him: *Burrows Ferret, Shamrock & Burrows, Detectives.*

"Miss Shamrock, this is scarcely necessary. I have yet to prove my value as your assistant, let alone your partner."

"Oh, Mr. Burrows, you're already proven! With your qualities, I'm surprised that you weren't a partner at Nutmeg and Bergamont."

"In point of fact, Miss Shamrock—"

"Please no more discussion, Mr. Burrows, over something so simple. The position is yours if you will have it. I feel the change is in our best interest. If you know a reason otherwise, I shall not insist."

"Thank you for your confidence, Miss Shamrock. I accept the honor and the responsibility."

To the young detective's relief, Burrows Ferret had taken over the media cases, freeing her from the routine of Interview, Analyze, Verify and Correct.

IAVC, staple of the detective business. In the rush to press, in their zeal to satisfy curiosity, newsferrets did not always confirm a story so much as they could, before setting it to print. The more interesting the story, in fact, and the more intriguing, the less likely it was to be true.

First, claimed the media, readers want to know. Second, all in good time, readers want to know the truth.

That a fascinating story may not be accurate was the bread and butter of detective ferrets, their names appearing often on the *Not Quite So* page of the daily papers.

There had been a story in the morning news, for instance, and a headline: *Stilton Ferret Risks Life to Save Kit's Doll from Avalanche.*

No sooner had the paper hit the streets than Burrows answered the telephone. "Shamrock and Burrows, at your service."

He listened. "I understand," he said. "Of course we can."

He penciled notes on his pad. "It will be done, Miss Yvette. Thank you for engaging us to resolve the issue."

Shamrock looked up from the Case of the Invisible Clock . . . how could a ferret vanish from his home in the city and reappear on the other side of the continent, no recollection of his disappearance or how he had traveled?

"Anything interesting, Mr. Burrows?"

"Yes, ma'am, as a matter of fact. That was MusTelCo's corporate office. Stockholders are calling: they saw the headline this morning. Is the world's richest ferret so reckless that he gambles his life and the future of his company to recover a stuffed animal?"

The shadow of a smile; in an instant she had analyzed the case. "Did Stilton Ferret Save Kit's Doll from Avalanche?"

"He did."

"Did Stilton Ferret Risk Life, doing it?"

"Stilton saw the kit drop her penguin in the snow when the warning sounded; he recovered the doll, returned it. The avalanche came downhill next day. I'll confirm this, of course, with the kit and her parents, and the ski patrol. Our correction will say that the penguin is safe, little Eliza is grateful and Stilton's life was at no time at risk."

She nodded. "Thank you, Mr. Burrows." Why would the world's biggest corporation, she wondered, call the world's smallest detective agency with such an important correction?

"My pleasure, Miss Shamrock."

He touched the flower on his desk, added water to its vase. Shamrock stiffened.

The *museum*! She had seen the old painting's vase in the museum!

But the museum was huge, city blocks under one roof. *Where* in the museum?

Somewhere, somewhere, said her recollection. Don't tell me, I'll get it. Same building, a different floor from the painting.

CHAPTER 8

She rushed into the Museum of Ancient Times
nearly at dusk, hurried down the Hall of Paintings
till she stood breathless, waiting, before the scene
that had so drawn her the day before.

The canvas waited, a cry without words, as though
painting were pantomime. Then the young ferret
sighed. So close. Something . . . she couldn't put
her paw upon the answer.

Gradually faded the light in the windows above the prehistoric work as day turned through sunset. She stood and studied, the detective a living net beneath the art, await for its clue to fall.

Night darkened, nearly to the shade of the painting's polka-dot tapestry. Minutes more, and it was as though the painting had changed to match the sky.

Shamrock Ferret blinked, transfixed by the scene. The fur of her tail stood straight.

That isn't a tapestry behind the vase, she thought, it's night sky. Those are no polka dots, they're *stars*—that's *Mustella,* the constellation of the Great Ferret! This oval frame is no country window, *it's the viewport of a starship!*

Her paw flew to her magnifying glass, she stepped forward, leaned to the painting, focused the lens. There, barely discernible around the oval, amid the cracks of ancient color, lay the faintest spots of an automatic welding machine, bonding frame to bulkhead.

Ten millionth visitor to this art, Shamrock Ferret was first to understand. Painter unknown, a smile across the ages: the flowers are Shooting Stars, dear viewer, and the polka dots are home.

Centuries, it's been with us, thought Shamrock, every day the answer in plain sight.

And the vase, that vase . . .

Her recollection powers blinked awake. *Early Artifacts!* Sorry it took so long. Fourth floor. You see, there are actually a number of vases that have caught your interest, and we had to sort the ancient one from . . .

"Fourth floor!" said Shamrock aloud, rushed past late-going visitors, heading for Early Artifacts, impatient with the stately rise of the elevator, the gentle opening of its door.

Her paws slid to a stop on polished marble, in front of a glass enclosure. There stood the vase of the painting, unruffled by sudden discovery.

Barely a paw high, it gave instant scale to the painting downstairs. The viewport, then, must have been three paws high at most, and two wide, suggesting a craft smaller than legend. The ship to bring the first ferrets to Earth was not a giant among the stars, thought Shamrock, it had been the size of a ferryboat!

There was a sign by the glass case: *Replicas of the artifacts are available at the museum store. If you wish to borrow an original artifact, please return it at your earliest convenience.*

Back by dawn, she promised, lifting the vase and leaving her business card where it had stood: *Shamrock Ferret, Shamrock & Burrows, Detectives.*

By the time she trotted up the steps to her flat, she was deep in mystery. She had asked, coincidence had given her the painting for an answer.

"What do the patterns mean?" *We come from the stars!*

CHAPTER 9

Is there still a way to save the world? thought Avedoi Merek. Is anyone left who wants to save it?

The philosopher ferret surveyed the remains of
the city through what had once been the window of
his study, now a jagged hole in the side of this modest villa, books and scrolls and disks tumbled about
within, smoke and flames scattered to the horizon
for Ferra's sunset.

We've defended ourselves nearly to death, he thought, and lacking miracles we're going to topple on over, defending to the last.

He sank into his thinking chair, its fabric torn by falling plasters.

What miracle, no assumptions beyond ferrets are intelligent, we're practical, curious, we love to laugh, we love adventure? What simple idea can save us now?

They ask me to speak to what's left of the world, as though . . .

He sighed, exhaling hope. What can I say, what can any creature say, to change the course of history after such a war as this?

It is

    just,

       too,

          late.

CHAPTER 10

Shamrock Ferret settled in her Cases Unsolved chair, smoothed her tail about her. She held the ferretmetal vase, lustrous silvery blue, in her paws and closed her eyes, remembering not to think, to allow its scenes to come to her unbidden.

Just let the story happen, whatever I need to learn from this vase. Just let it be . . .

⌢

It was a room, Shamrock saw, once a comfortable library, a grand view over housetops to a soaring metropolis.

Now glass was blown from every window, shambles for furnishings, one wall gone, the view beyond of flames splashed near and distant, a city shattered.

She so shrank from this sight, a meteor storm across a living planet, that her body shivered in her worn chair, she nearly opened her eyes to stop the scene from coming.

She did not. For curled at a splintered desk was a smallish ferret, not much larger than Shamrock herself, fur the color of sand and night.

His eyes were closed, but she knew his thought.

So desperate are they now, that they ask me to speak to the world, prisoner become savior. What words can save? I am one animal, I watch the end of civilization as I know it. It is just, too, late.

In her imagination, she stepped toward him, and at the sound, his eyes opened. "Who are . . ."

". . . you?" they asked together.

"My name is Shamrock," she said. "I'm from . . ." She stopped, not knowing how to tell him where she was from.

She was to him a flickering hologram; through her body could he see the fires on the horizon. And yet she lived. Was she some alien race, arrived past its chance to save the life of his world?

He nodded. "I'm the last of ferret civilization," he told her, "one of the last. You came to rescue us from ourselves. You found only Avedoi Merek, and the end."

Shamrock blinked, unbelieving. "Avedoi Merek? I found *Avedoi Merek*?"

He looked through the missing wall, turned back to Shamrock. "Ferra will go on. Our planet will barely notice we're gone. A small irritation vanished, the race of ferrets."

"Avedoi Merek! Sir, you're not the end, you're the—"

"Would it have been so difficult," said the other, unhearing, "just to have been kind to each other? Why must ferrets be the only animal cursed with this magnetism toward hatreds and putting-downs, we're-number-one, us-against-them?"

Shamrock gaped, astonished at the fires surrounding. "Meteors?"

The philosopher tilted his head, puzzled that the alien didn't guess.

"No meteors." He touched his chest. "The disaster wasn't out there, it was in here. One side thought, 'We're good, you're evil.' The other side thought, 'No, you have it wrong: *we're* good, *you're* evil!'"

How could this remarkable animal joke in such a moment, she thought, fires still burning? Not funny. "*Evil ferrets?* What are you saying, sir?"

He didn't hear. "The war began, each side convinced we can harm others without harming ourselves and the ones we love. Can't be done." He shrugged. "Can't be done."

The philosopher roused himself. "Highest perspective, of course: it doesn't matter. We are indestructible light, all of us. Dying out of bodies is as much a dream as living in them. Change the dream to nightmare, though, it's no fun. We're the most fun-loving animal in the universe! Why would we choose this tragedy, to hurt each other, to hurt ourselves and our kits?"

The room swirled, Shamrock understanding at last. "War?" she whispered. "Between *ferrets*?"

Avedoi Merek nodded, studied her closely. "You're from another star, aren't you?" It was not her appearance he saw, but her attitude, her shock at what she had heard.

"No," he said. "You're not from another place, you're from another time. Our destruction wouldn't surprise if you were from the past. You're from the future."

"Yes," she said. "No. I'm dreaming. I'm imagining."

"Aren't we all. And the race of ferrets has imagined its own ending. Now we've decided to end dreams in war against each other." He looked to Shamrock, as though for hope. "Haven't we?"

"Sir, I can't believe . . ." She struggled to explain the obvious, frustrated that this brilliant animal could not understand: ferrets do not fight wars.

"*The Courtesies!*" she said. "Avedoi Merek, it was you who set them down! How could there be war . . . *what happened to the Courtesies?*"

The philosopher watched her for the longest time before he spoke.

"What courtesies?"

CHAPTER 11

To any client who might have opened her door, Shamrock Ferret was asleep in her Cases Unsolved chair, nose tucked under her paw, a ball of warm sable encircling an ancient vase. Anyone entering would have stopped at the sight, held their breath and tiptoed away, closing the door silently behind.

The detective, however, was not asleep. Lured by the mystery of ferretkind's distant past, her breathing was quick and shallow as she watched events in this state that any other would call trance.

"*What Courtesies?*" she cried. "Avedoi Merek, you wrote them! *The Ferret Way*! Your book is so ancient that some say you never existed, your name's a code we all forgot!"

The philosopher smiled the faintest of smiles. "My dear strange visitor, have you come to the wrong address? *The Ferret Way* is a title and some notes, nothing more. An idea, a path that could have been, but for . . ."

He moved his paw toward the scene outside, the fires in the night. "Too late. It will never be written. Could-have-been is fiction, now."

Shamrock refused to surrender. "Aren't you baffled?" she said. "Don't you wonder how I can appear before you out of the air, your hallucination of the future who happens to know every line of a book unwritten, it's just notes in your mind? Has this . . ." she searched for the word ". . . war destroyed your curiosity? Have I found the wrong address? Is there *another* Avedoi Merek?"

"The future," said the animal, as though speaking that word for the first time. "If you're my future, then for all its . . ." He blinked at her. "The war is not the end of the world!"

Shamrock felt brittle tension cracking away. "My time, sir, we've *forgotten* your war! My time, war's unimaginable. Because of you. *The Ferret Way,* it's so deep in our culture we're incapable of war. Don't you remember? *Who reads, loves, lives the Ferret Way becomes keeper of light, ennobling outer worlds from one within!*"

"You've set a civilization on a book I haven't written! I don't know those ideas myself. How can I find them out?"

"That's easy enough," said Shamrock, desperate. "I'll tell you!"

The animal at the desk stared at her, stunned in paradox. Then, for the first time since before the rockets had fallen over Ferra, Avedoi Merek laughed.

CHAPTER 12

"You don't remember, sir?" Shamrock Ferret stood by a shattered window-wall that had once lifted seamless from rooftops far below, knowing she dreamed, unafraid of the height.

"'Not laws,' you said, sir, 'not rules': 'Here is a constitution of courtesies, should you choose to live by them. The courtesy you show to those you love, show the same to all, be you a civilization of one . . .'"

Avedoi Merek wrote on scorched paper in the ancient Ferrune, his own words echoing from a reader generations removed.

". . . or of millions," he whispered as Shamrock fell silent, watching. He wrote as though in trance himself.

". . . these courtesies to self and others will be your justice, lifting you beyond strife and destructions, now and forever."

He no longer cared about too late, about hopeless, no longer despaired what one animal could say to a shattered planet. Letters flew beneath his paws, listing the Courtesies without so much as slowing, one to the next:

Whatever harm I would do to another, I shall do first to myself.

As I respect and am kind to myself, so shall I respect and be kind to peers, to elders, to kits.

I claim for others the freedom to live as they wish, to think and believe as they will. I claim that freedom for myself.

I shall make each choice and live each day to my highest sense of right.

Shamrock stood fascinated, a silent witness. The Courtesies were so fundamental to her race that many insisted they were not declaration but ferret nature, genetic code. Now, word by word, she watched the ideas written.

Avedoi Merek looked up to her, his eyes alight. "Of course!" he murmured. "As we shift our energy from destructions, where can it go but to adventure instead? Instead of turning rockets on ourselves, we change their direction—into the stars, us aboard!"

She nodded, and the facts came together. We came to Earth from space. The painting, the vase she held this moment in her office, art it was but history more. And history had begun with one animal, with this gentle ferret before her.

"Is it true?" she asked. "We have a legend about you."

The philosopher smiled. A legend about one so humble as himself?

"In the archives," said Shamrock, "I found a story. It said that Avedoi Merek once was asked what he would do if he knew he was to be attacked by warriors."

"Oh? By warriors? What did I answer?"

"'Die.'"

He laughed. "Good for me. At last I learned to stop fighting."

"Is the story true?"

"No."

What's true, thought Shamrock, is the idea behind the story: when every noble, gentle creature refuses to fight, nobility and gentility will disappear before warriors. All that will remain, at the end, will be an angry few, gnashing their hatreds in the ruins of a silent planet.

"You're changing the world," she said. "Can you feel it, now, do you know it as you write?"

Preoccupied, the animal spoke just above a whisper. "I change nothing, Miss Shamrock. Ferrets change when we decide a new way of thinking will make us happier than an old one. No other way. We're too stubborn. I write to change myself."

It felt to Shamrock as if she were a spirit no longer required in this place. She had reminded one animal of what it knew, and now it wrote for others who might someday care.

She woke in her Cases Unsolved chair, reached at once to her notepad.

Her psychic voyage had offered a clue to one moment, about which the destiny of a civilization had turned. Not ferret nature, said the dream, not genetic code. Once, long ago, we changed our minds: end violence. In its place, no matter what: courtesy.

A sensitive's fable or a civilization's history?

CHAPTER 13

"Would you care for tea, Miss Shamrock?"

"Why, yes, thank you, Mr. Burrows."

He brought the china, poured her Mandalay and a swirl of honey. "Difficult case?"

She nodded, and he left her to her deduction. So deep ran the Courtesies that Burrows saw in her nod how warm his kindness felt to her, how glad she was that he was there.

She sipped the tea, staring at a fringe of carpet.

"Mr. Burrows," she said.

He appeared at once. "Yes, Miss Shamrock?"

"I need your help."

"Of course."

The fluffy animal settled himself in the Cases Resolved chair nearby, turned to her and said not another word.

Shamrock thought for a long while, her partner silent. "I saw Avedoi Merek and the ferret war," she said at last. "I saw him write the Courtesies."

Burrows did not respond. "I need your help," to ferrets, means, "Please listen." No comments, no suggestions, no debate. Just listen.

"But seeing is not proof. How do I know it happened?"

Her partner listened.

"War between ferrets, Mr. Burrows? Not likely. We're smart enough, we don't need disaster to learn kindness."

Silence for minutes. "And yet, if there had been war, and ferrets overcame it, we need to know! If I could prove it was a choice, we made . . ."

Burrows listened.

"One does not war against friends," she said. "At some point we decided: all ferrets are friends. Us-and-Them changed to Us."

Long silence, her eyes closed. "If that deciding happened not slowly, over a million years, but in the minute I saw Avedoi Merek lift his pen . . . that's not dumb genetics, Mr. Burrows, that's one animal and an idea!"

Burrows nodded, Shamrock didn't see.

"And if that's true, the power of one animal and an idea," she said, "how many other walls are out there, painted invisible, holding us back, waiting for us to wake up?"

The clock ticked.

"Evidence, Mr. Burrows! Nothing I saw can I prove. Did I witness some golden deed that picked up history and set it on different tracks? Or was I imagining fiction?"

At last she turned to him, said her test in a word. "Evidence."

He listened.

"I'm done, Mr. Burrows. Thank you for your help."

The other animal reached a paw and brushed his whiskers. "An honor to listen, Miss Shamrock. You have a remarkable mind."

He rose and padded softly to his desk.

"Comments, Mr. Burrows? Where is my thinking weak?"

He lifted a cup of tea gone cool. "You're a sensitive, Miss Shamrock, your psychometry has proven itself so far. To the best of my knowledge, it has never been meaningless, is that true?"

"So far."

"Some will question the paradox, of course. If we travel to the past and give an author ideas he has not yet written, where did the ideas come from, us or him?"

"Him, of course. Multiple worlds."

"I'm afraid I haven't studied that branch of mystery, Miss Shamrock."

"I was telling him his own ideas. But as soon as he saw me, the world split away from the world in which he didn't see me. In one world, he writes the Courtesies alone, in the other, a vision reminds him. Not one past and future, Burrows, many pasts, many futures. No paradox."

"I must study, indeed," said her partner, his eyes twinkling. "I suppose there are worlds in which I study, and in which I don't. In which I put off studying . . ."

Shamrock nodded, solemn. "Every possible variation of every possible variable. Every decision separates the universe from what it would have been without it."

"I trust that we have now entered the universe in which Miss Shamrock Ferret solves the very mystery of our origins."

She looked to him, saw the twinkle in his eyes and laughed. "One of those universes, I hope!"

Shamrock reached to the ancient vase, touched it softly. She closed her eyes.

CHAPTER 14

It was a stage, she saw, a raised circular platform, brighter than the dim about. It stood before an auditorium of seats empty save for herself. Beyond the seats, a council chamber.

Inlaid, high on a wall of dark wood, a silver map of the planet Ferra. Beneath it, the harsh figure of a two-headed creature, a winged serpent, emerald green, thunderbolts in one claw, arrows in the other.

Beneath the serpent stood a wide, curving desk, places there for nine governors; in four of them sat ferrets of varying furs and masks but of one defeated countenance. Each wore a black scarf, and an emblem affixed, the emerald serpent.

As Shamrock looked about her in the empty place, Avedoi Merek entered and walked down the aisle of the auditorium, alone. The gentle animal stepped to the center of the platform, stood quietly in his white scarf, the emblem of the serpent pinned at his throat.

An unimposing figure, she thought, no chiseled features, no penetrating gaze, yet about him . . . it was as though, when he took the stage, some great magnet energized.

As the remains of ferret civilization watched, the philosopher faced a world's cameras and the surviving members of his nation's council.

"You will forgive me if I am not so eloquent or entertaining this evening," he said. "I have little to say, but perhaps I speak for most us still alive."

He studied the remaining leaders, looked into the cameras beyond them to survivors on every corner of the globe.

"From this day forth," he said, and then he paused for the longest while, "I withdraw my consent from evil."

The words echoed from speakers in halls and homes and public spaces.

I withdraw my consent from evil. Any other time, the idea would have been a puzzle, a trick of words. Today, however, Avedoi Merek became the voice of a civilization's conscience, stark and straight, and today a race of animals listened.

"I withdraw my consent," he said, "from war." Soft-spoken, an impossibility all of a sudden required.

"I withdraw my consent from violence," said Merek. "From hatred. From malice."

He looked into the heart of every one of his race left alive.

"I withdraw my consent from these. In my actions. In my thought. In my choices."

He reached to the emerald serpent pinned at his throat, unfastened it, let it fall. "I withdraw my consent from evil. Forever."

Once there would have been a flicker of lights across the map of the continent, protest from those needing to argue definition and circumstance, to cry for patriotism. Now, after what had happened, the map was still.

An entire society with the freedom and the power to destroy itself listened, numbed at how close it had come to doing so.

"We have one chance to save ourselves and our future. There is one way, and it is so simple that it is impossible."

Watching, some ferrets fancied that they could see light around the face of this gentle creature, once chained and jailed, enemy of the state for speaking against a ferret war. The first hearts felt hope glimmer in darkness.

"May I ask?" he said. "Who has enjoyed our experiment with destruction? Who is happy for what has happened?" Two questions, and silence.

Enjoyed? the ferrets thought, smoke still rising from ruins about them. *Happy?*

Here the image faded, spiraled out of reach, and Shamrock blinked awake in her Cases Unsolved chair.

She shook herself, as much to shudder away the weight of the old time as to clear her mind of the image. She set the blue-metal vase gently on the table alongside her chair.

He had told her the truth, she thought. There had come the end of the world, and the one who rose against it was Avedoi Merek.

Have I stumbled into some different past, she thought, an ice-warped Ferra from might-have-been? She rubbed her eyes, stirred uneasily in the chair.

He called us to our highest right.

Different pasts, maybe. But could there have been a violent Before in the past we know today? She shivered. No history had hinted such a thing.

Ever have ferrets been creatures of warmth and courtesy. Always have we loved action and adventure, always we've been willing to overcome fear and to face peril along the paths that we've chosen.

Yet Shamrock trembled at what she had seen. That was no alternate past, it had been herself from today carried back to Avedoi Merek's demolished home, herself in the council chamber, her own heart singed, so near the arson of a civilization.

The vase stood silent on the table by her chair as if it were watching her, wondering why she had come to learn what no one else remembered.

Either ferret history is wrong, she thought, or my psychic powers have turned more dark and destructive than any creature's, ever.

She engaged the mystery, could not resolve it.

In all *The Paws of Knowledge,* in every ancient scroll and passage, not a word of war between ferrets. Ferrets can be mistaken, but they do not lie. Could it happen that somehow an entire culture *forgot* what once had been?

With a start she heard the clock chime dawn. She had agreed to return the vase to the museum at her earliest convenience. That was now. She lifted the ancient art and hurried to the museum.

It was light when she removed her business card and set the vase gently behind its glass, but she could not shake from her mind the gloom of the violence she had seen. Cities had been turned to fire, lives of peers and elders—lives of kits!—had been lost.

Ferrets don't ruin, she thought, her steps whispering on the early sidewalk, past shops asleep, undefended, no locks for their doors. We don't harm, we don't destroy. Even the suggestion—*an unkind ferret*—it makes one smile. Every ferret respects every other, lives always to its highest right. It is our way.

Were she any other creature, Shamrock Ferret would have shivered and put the whole strange scene from her mind, studied her next case and never looked back. But for this creature, the impossible was mystery, and mystery must always be resolved.

CHAPTER 15

Her solution that week to the Case of the Invisible Clock provoked a flurry of attention in the press, stories for a few days that Burrows needed to correct.

His release to the newsferrets explained that contrary to speculation, Shamrock Ferret was not accomplished in sorcery, she was not a master illusionist, she did not possess a bionic brain.

"Miss Shamrock," he wrote, "is extraordinary in that she is a careful observer of ferrets and scenes, she has a retentive memory, she considers alternate possibilities and she applies established principles of deduction to her business, which is to detect that which is overlooked by others."

All of this was true. Shamrock noticed. And so she noticed, not long after Burrows had come to work with her, that she had been earning somewhat more attention from the press than she had before. She found the timing odd, discounted it.

MusTelCo, for instance, could have gone to any qualified detective to correct an erring headline, she thought. The giant company hadn't sent a card and a kit's stuffed penguin to thank Burrows for publicizing Shamrock Ferret, but for getting the corporation out of hot water. A little publicity is normal, she thought. When one deals with mysteries, one must not be surprised at the interest of inquiring minds.

Haunting her now was the much bigger puzzle that no one had hired her to solve: the Case of the Golden Deed. Did one ferret change history? If he did, how could she prove it?

Anyone watching Shamrock would have smiled, that afternoon. For an hour her fluffy body lay motionless, fast asleep in the bedroom above the office. Next instant blankets flying, lights aflare, the ferret diving from her hammock, fur awry, hooking a scarf as she bolted downstairs and out the door.

"Good afternoon, Miss Shamrock," said Burrows as the door slammed shut.

The mystery's not what happened before Avedoi Merek stood in the cameras of Ferra, thought Shamrock, running toward the museum, it's *what happened after*! The answer's still in the vase!

Panting from her run, she burst out of the fourth-floor elevator. Sometimes the best you can do is not-think. So many levels of the mind . . .

She had opened the glass door of the case before she realized that what she had come for was no longer there. The spot where the vase had stood was empty save for a business card:

Nutmeg Ferret
Nutmeg & Bergamont, Detectives

CHAPTER 16

Shamrock bent over the antiquities display and listened to the silence while it roared in her ears. No, she thought. Something is wrong. Coincidence helps us, coincidence does not block our way. How can it be that it's *gone*?

She returned to the elevator, rode in no hurry to the main floor, walked out the door and down the steps to the sidewalk, her puzzlement more real than the city around her.

If coincidence helps, she thought, how am I helped that the world's most famous detective has borrowed my vase at the very hour I need it myself? The question was a mini-case itself, and her inner observer stood apart, watched her solve it.

Does Nutmeg Ferret know I want the vase?
    Assume yes.
Has she taken the vase to help me?
    Assume yes.
How am I helped, if I miss the vase?
    No answer.
What do I learn from not having the vase?
    No answer.

Eyes down, watching the sidewalk, the detective sniffed in frustration. Her inner observer smiled.

If I learn—something—why should Nutmeg Ferret, whom I have ever admired and never met, care?
    Because I matter to her.
Why do I matter to her?
    Wrong question.
Is it Nutmeg alone? What of the shadowy Bergamont?
    Wrong question.

Burrows would know the answer, she thought, but it would not be ethical for me to ask after his former employers. She set her jaw. *There is nothing I cannot detect on my own, without help.*

She swept her mind clean, started over.

Why do I need the vase?
Because it is soaked in the images of centuries ago, and I can unlock those images when I hold it in my paws.

Good answer! she thought. Follow it, follow it!

Is what I need to know outside of me?
No.
Does empty matter contain knowledge that I do not?
No!
Why do I need the vase?
It helps me see what I already know.
Why do I need its help?

The mystery felt Shamrock closing on it highspeed. It leaped aside, darted for cover, not fast enough. Quick as a shadow the detective closed her paw, seized it in a flash, midair. It sighed, smiled at her: "Nice catch, Shamrock!"

Why do I need its help? Sometimes, unless you start over, you'll never start at all.

By the time she reached home, Shamrock Ferret was running again. She flew up the steps, threw open the door, her partner looking up startled from his desk.

She trembled excitement. "Thought experiment, Mr. Burrows! Imagine a report in *Ferret Science* magazine. Two tests of the accuracy of psychometry: one with the sensitive holding an object, one with the sensitive holding a *substitute* for the same object! Which test is more accurate?"

She threw her hat and scarf toward the wall. Both missed their pegs, tumbled to the floor. She retrieved them, paced the office. Why do you take so long, Mr. Burrows?

"Why, they're the *same,* Miss Shamrock. Bless my whiskers, what an interesting experiment! The reason, you see, is that the information they seek—"

"—is not in the object, it's in the *sensitive!*"

She leaped headlong to her Cases Unsolved chair.

"Mr. Burrows, bring me something!"

"Of course, Miss Shamrock. What would you like?"

"Anything! Something I can hold."

A smile, and he offered MusTelCo's stuffed penguin.

She looked up to him, smiled back, glad for his calm. "Thank you. I suppose I might settle down a bit."

"There's nothing wrong with adventure, Miss Shamrock."

With this, Burrows, ever thoughtful, bade her good evening and departed in white scarf and tweed hat. Shamrock heard the purr of his Austin-Furet starting, easing away into the streets. Then she took the penguin in her paws, settled properly in her chair, relaxed and closed her eyes.

"I hold a vase," she whispered, "from an ancient time . . ."

The first image came clear at once: a ferret kit, all dusty sable, grasped a fluffy cloth penguin in its teeth, dragged it toward a playpen tunnel.

The detective opened her eyes. "Hm . . ."

Three deep breaths, she thought. Body relaxed. Mind relaxed. I am in the council chamber . . .

Flash of a penguin diving, then darkness swirling around her. Let go, she thought, let the image offer itself.

Then, no warning, instant clarity:

A penguin stood upon the lighted platform, facing the remains of the council under the scowl of the two-headed serpent. Shamrock murmured, and the penguin dissolved to the form of a ferret, the color of sand and night.

"Who has enjoyed our experiment with destruction? Who is happy for what has happened?" Avedoi Merek stood alone before a planet's cameras, asked the questions into silence.

"If we are not happy," the words slow, uninterrupted, "if our experiment has brought us not well-being but pain and loss and horror, must we, ever? repeat it."

Not a sound in the chamber, not one response light on the map of the planet. By his presence alone did this creature command the attention of survivors everywhere.

At once a cloud of penguins fluttered and soared, squawking, stark tuxedos in the air, turning and diving through the scene, shredding the moment.

"No," said Shamrock upon her chair, unsmiling, firm, tenacious to watch. "Let this continue! *Without interruption . . .*"

The penguins vanished, squawks echoing away.

"I am a simple animal," said Avedoi Merek, "of more questions than answers. One of my questions is this: What would happen, if we accept for everyone, that constitution which we already accept for ourselves? Not laws, not rules.

"Here is a constitution of *courtesies,* should we choose to live by them. The courtesy we show to those we love, show the same to all, be we a civilization of one or of millions:

"Whatever harm I would do to another, I shall do first to myself.

"As I respect and am kind to myself, so shall I respect and be kind to peers, to elders, to kits.

"I claim for others the freedom to live as they wish, to think and believe as they will. I claim that freedom for myself.

"I shall make each choice and live each day to my highest sense of right."

As though he were an alchemist alone in some dark workshop, Avedoi Merek transmuted pain and terror into resolution. His words were neither plea nor demand—one creature stood before the rest and made a personal decision, invited his race to join him if it wished.

Watching, eyes closed, Shamrock Ferret had changed from observer to witness. Whether any other walks with him, she thought, I will. In trance, she waited for him to continue the list of courtesies by which her culture lived to this day. *I take the name Ferret,* she murmured, *to declare always that I am not rival or enemy, but of one family . . .*

But the animal who stood before the council and the cameras of his world was silent.

At last, nearly a whisper: ". . . thank you." The ferret nodded to himself. He had forgotten nothing. "Thank you."

Then he turned and stepped from the platform, walked away. He glanced toward Shamrock, nodded as though he felt her presence more than saw it.

A door opened to an outside hallway, the shadow of a penguin beyond. Avedoi Merek passed through, the door closed.

In her trance, Shamrock saw a few scattered lights begin to flicker upon the map of the planet, then more, and then yet more. Hundreds and hundreds of lights.

CHAPTER 17

It was true, thought Shamrock. The answers we seek are not outside us, but within. Psychometry, like every other science, is a tool to find what we already know. Artifacts help because we believe they will help.

When Burrows arrived next morning, Shamrock was curled on the sofa, reviewing her notes of the evening past.

If it was true that ferrets had been violent creatures who chose to give up violence, she thought, the change in civilization more likely happened all at once, from one traumatic event, than from a few laying down arms before others.

Avedoi Merek had said so himself: "If some choice has brought us horror, must we, ever? repeat it."

That instant, thought Shamrock, *that* was the moment we changed.

Now: What possible proof could exist that what she had imagined was real? Where was her evidence?

The detective stayed up late, built a nest of heavy volumes, most of her *Paws of Knowledge* around her, massive butterflies circling her Cases Unsolved chair.

Then she was off to the library, a few of the volumes surrounding printed in the ancient Ferrune. What she found was a blank wall.

There is no mention in any record, anywhere, of any war, ever in history. No battles, no dates of combat, no victory or defeat, nothing but peace and harmony through the history of the race of ferretkind, since the beginning.

But I saw it! I saw the ruins of cities, hope destroyed in rubble and fire. I saw Avedoi Merek speak to the world! How could I imagine that, from nothing, no precedent in all the records of my race?

CHAPTER 18

"Would you care for tea, Miss Shamrock?"

"Yes, thank you, Mr. Burrows, I would."

In that moment the engine-telegraph doorbell rang, the handle moved from *Engines Standby* to *Ahead Full,* then back again.

"Come in, please," said Burrows.

There was no response, no sound from bell or door. He poured tea and honey, set the service down, crossed the room and opened the door.

"Bless my whiskers," he muttered. "There's no one here!"

He looked left and right onto the street outside, saw no one. Then he looked down, stooped to the threshold, lifted a sheet of metal foil, silvery blue. "Hello . . ."

The big ferret blinked at strange markings, shook his head, looked once more down the street. Then he closed the door, walked to Shamrock and set the foil before her. "I'm afraid I'm a little rusty on my ancient alphabets."

Shamrock frowned a question at him: Ancient alphabets?

Not printed, was the sheet, but rather illuminated in gold, fine-wrought vines curling around the margin, trumpet-flowers of royal purple encircling the page.

In the center, lettered by paw, shining Ferrune calligraphy:

⁂

Shamrock was not rusty on her Ferrune, she loved the old characters.

> *"In the moat, which is Loch Stoat,"* she read,
>> *A strange petal flowers.*
>> *What is the pollen for?*
>>> *S.*

As she held the foil, she closed her eyes, called images forth. Flash of a meteor through the night, a sunken ship, a blossom opening beneath the waves. And then, odd sight, an image of herself, as in a mirror, smiling.

That no one waited on her doorstep was not astonishing. Tips and clues from those who did not wish to be known were normal in her business. Ferrets are curious about others, modest about themselves—so thrived their television and tabloids. But why this peculiar message, and whose the initial at the bottom?

Why would someone want anonymously to offer a clue, and if clue it was, to which of her cases did it apply?

She set the foil down. "What do you make of it, Mr. Burrows?"

"It's ferretmetal, Miss Shamrock."

Indeed, she thought. And . . . ?

"Someone would like you to make a journey."

"To Loch Stoat."

"So it would seem."

"To do what?"

A long silence. "My guess, Miss Shamrock, is that you intend to find out."

Once he had joined Shamrock Ferret, the courtesy of ethics had broken Burrows' contact with Nutmeg and the firm for which he had worked. If they were behind this, he thought, whatever they had planned they had done it without his knowledge or consent.

CHAPTER 19

Her research changed at once, turned on Loch Stoat.

The earliest reference she found was written in Ferrune, a sonnet on the building of the palace upon its shores; the latest was a fantasy by kits writer Budgeron Ferret. Fantasy, however, she thought, entering the Ebon Mask bookstore, is not meaningless.

She found a little chair in the kits' section of the bookstore, sat there and read Budgeron's book through before she bought it.

A serpent in Loch Stoat, indeed. But a very different sort of serpent, as Budgie and his friend Bvuhlgahri Bat had discovered, one with a gift that could change their time. Was it fiction, the writer's imagination overlapping her own, or could a serpent beneath the waters of the loch be a clue in the Case of the Golden Deed?

CHAPTER 20

Burrows drove the distance from London, the Austin-Furet purring happily at speeds only an expert driver could manage.

Shamrock held her breath, once, in the highlands, gripped the paw-hold as the roadster drifted high power around a tighter turn than most.

"I'd hold on, too," he told her, "in any other machine. But the Furet and I, we've driven our share of rallies, a bit more challenging than the F3 to Scotland. Safety is control, Miss Shamrock, no matter speed, and control is something I've . . ." He glanced at her. "Would you care to slow a little, ma'am?"

The detective released her grip, relaxed her body from nose to tail. "As fast as you dare, Mr. Burrows."

Her partner laughed, admiring the young detective. The Furet took the next turn with a little less torque, and without the drift.

By afternoon the two ferrets motored slowly through the grounds of the palace at Mustelania. Bright flags flew in sunlight from the towers, kits and grown-ups picnicked and played on the broad lawns and parks. Groups joined together, tours through the vast basements of the palace itself, the largest library on earth.

Adjoining the palace to the east glittered the waters of Loch Stoat. Burrows navigated traffic till they arrived at the shore, then as others turned left to follow the highway north, he angled right onto a grassy lane, stopped by a waterfront restaurant.

"Hungry, Miss Shamrock?" he said. "Perhaps a late lunch before we're off to sea? I highly recommend the crêpes flambé."

Odd, thought Shamrock. How is it that Burrows could be such a regular customer so far north?

The maître d' nodded to Burrows, led the partners to a place overlooking the water, and though the restaurant was not crowded, Shamrock remarked that they had been given the best table in the house.

"I must say you deserve it, Miss Shamrock," said Burrows. "It's not every day that one solves such a case as yours."

She laughed. "It's a long way from solved. So far, the Golden Deed is in my mind, I'm afraid. We've come all this way on the hope of a clue that seems to be eluding us."

She recited once again what she had memorized the instant she had seen the metal scroll: "'*In the moat, which is Loch Stoat, a strange petal flowers. What is the pollen for?*' Sixteen words, Mr. Burrows, sixty-six characters."

"Eighty-one characters, counting spaces, ma'am. The number of words plus the number of letters equals the total number of characters."

She shook her head. "A dead end, I'm afraid. Six *A*'s, no *B*'s, two *C*'s, no *D*'s, six *E*'s . . . I don't believe it's a letter puzzle. It doesn't seem to be a number puzzle."

The waiter arrived, a handsome animal, pale fur, black paws and mask, scarf the color of the loch. "A fine choice," he said of their order. He looked with strange intensity at Shamrock, and a curious smile. "Would you care for our Mandalay tea, ma'am?"

She looked to him, startled. "Yes," she said, "yes, please."

"And honey. Poured, not stirred?"

She nodded, wordless.

"Of course, Miss Shamrock," and he left toward the kitchen.

"Mr. Burrows," she said, "what was that about?"

Her partner smiled. "What was what about?"

"'Miss Shamrock,' when I've never been here before."

He shrugged. "Solve the cases you've solved, your picture in the magazines, ma'am, it's not amazing you're becoming known, here and there."

"My picture in the magazines."

Her partner shrugged. "*Who's in the News,* that sort of thing. There have been some mentions.

Your cases are interesting, your ways. The up-and-coming detective, unique mind, that sort of thing. You may not choose to read about yourself, others do."

She shook off the implications, that is, the shattering change ahead should ever she shift from private animal to public.

Ferrets delight in their celebrities, their aristocracy of merit, its dukes and princesses chosen from every calling. If you excel at your craft, there is a good chance that curious ferrets will need to know why, to find what makes you different.

The kit Shamrock had been no exception, following Nutmeg Ferret's cases, eager to learn all she could of how her heroine's lightning mind worked, what she thought, how she lived.

Burrows watched sunlight on the loch, stretching blue and deep to mossy hills beyond, as silent at his place as though he were listening to his partner's hidden conversation.

Heaven help animals caught in the blaze of ferret curiosity, thought Shamrock, for they need the help of angels. Everyone lives to her or his own highest standard, erring from time to time, learning from errors; she was no different. Celebrity ferrets, though, are expected never to err.

No matter one's old calling, the new one, after a ferret catches the curiosity of others, is role model, example. For every animal, everywhere in the culture.

"Without the poetry," said Burrows, shattering her thoughts, "the scroll tells us this: Loch Stoat is protecting something that is odd and beautiful, which affects the world in ways we don't know. To solve your mystery, you've got to find out what that something is and what it does."

Shamrock frowned, shook her head. "Simpler than that, Mr. Burrows. If it's a clue to the Golden Deed, and I'm not sure it is, it's saying that what I need to know is in the loch. At the bottom of the loch, I suspect."

"And what is it that you need to know, Miss Shamrock?"

She smiled. The question was with her day and night. "Proof," she said. "Evidence. Without evidence, Shamrock Ferret's not solved anything, she's a psychic time traveler, telling stories."

"The proof's underwater?"

"I'll find it there, Mr. Burrows, or it's going to find me, on my way to the bottom."

Her partner startled at the words, as if she knew more than she was telling: *it will find me.*

She nodded, her highest right demanding a decision. "I'm going to be met," she said. "Whoever wrote that scroll expects me to come looking."

CHAPTER 21

She learns all she can, thought Burrows, she pours fact through experience, and then she leaps, trusting intuition. One must admire her courage. He nodded. Courage is the final test.

The *ScubaFerrets* boat arrowed toward the center of Loch Stoat, Shamrock listening to intuition, wishing the riddle might have been a little more specific about *where* in Loch Stoat its strange petal might flower.

Then without knowing why, she called, "Stop here, please!"

The captain smiled behind her sunglasses, reached her paw to the throttle. The boat slowed, stopped, reversed at idle power until Shamrock nodded. "That's fine, thank you, ma'am."

Then, engine off, the boat drifted on the rippled mirror of the lake.

"It's deep out here," said the captain, a ferret the color of charcoal, cap low over her eyes, scarf ruffled on the hint of a breeze. "There'd be a lot more to see near shore . . ."

"This will be fine, thank you."

Shamrock snapped the buckles of the diving harness about her, slipped on fins and weight belt and mask, tested her air supply. She fastened a reel of white line to her belt, lifted a sealed floodlight.

"Wait for me, please, Mr. Burrows," she said. "If I don't find an air supply down there, I'll be back before long. But I suspect . . ." She flashed him a look of delicious adventure. "If I'm not back by sunset, bring a light and follow my line."

"If you're not back, I'll be following sooner than that, Miss Shamrock."

High sun plunged spears of light into the water around the boat, the shafts gleaming near the surface, then fading away, no bottom in sight.

Shamrock stepped to the transom ladder, swung her paws free and dropped into the water. In that second she thought this might be a foolish idea, free-diving toward she didn't know what, expecting guidance to appear on its own.

She waved to Burrows, swept her fear aside. Not foolish. There is a case to be solved. Then she was gone, a sable form sinking through dark crystal.

"She won't see much, Mr. Burrows." The captain smiled at the detective's partner. "It's the deepest part of the loch. Why dive where there's nothing to see?"

CHAPTER 22

Shamrock turned as she sank, watching, a thousand bubbles trapped like bright pearls in her fur. Everything beyond was featureless blue mystery.

No floor below, not a fish to be seen, even the boat above disappeared from view. But for the dim line uncoiling from the reel at her belt and her own silver breath trailing upward, the detective could have been floating in space.

Three hundred paws down, the surface was a hazy direction in the dim, nothing more.

Now what, she thought, wait? Ferrets of action do not wait. I've got enough air to go to the bottom, but not to explore. Touch down, a few minutes for a square search and it will be time to come up again, decompressing along the way.

She switched the floodlight on, dropped lower. Looking down, darkness, the beam fetching out twenty paws into gloom then swallowed up in nothing.

Down she sank, descending at a speed she reckoned would give her a few seconds' warning before she hit the bottom.

Now through her beam darted a single silver flash, smaller than a minnow, flying upward. Then another in its trail, glittering briefly in Shamrock's light. They showed no curiosity about her, did not stop or circle as fish might have circled about a diver. They're not so much fish, she thought, as insects on some mission. Underwater insects? she wondered. *Aqua-bees?*

Then there it was, the floor of the lake, all of a sudden surrounding her so far as her beam could penetrate.

A bottom not jagged rock but smooth as a platter, a cloud of silt rising up where her paws touched. Images fluttered as she touched, rapid-clicking, a deck of picture cards shuffled, and stopped on the last, an arching bow of color.

Her paws slid on the surface, which curved gently downward to her left. The farther she slid, the steeper the curve, till she kicked free and free-fell once more beside this boulder towering into the dark.

A second landing, and Shamrock stood upon what seemed to be a floor of matted grass.

She swept her light beneath the boulder. At the end of the sweep a sudden sparkle glinted back, reflected from midnight.

The great shape did not rest on the bottom, she noticed, but some ten paws above it, as though supported by rock. There was room underneath to stand, to walk for some distance.

The detective did not think as much as she watched, gathering information. She could not stay long.

The reflection glittered from her light as she approached, till it shimmered like quicksilver overhead, an air pocket beneath this sleeping giant.

A dim form touched her in the darkness, and she bolted back, spun the light upon it. The form was silent, unmoving. The form was a steel ladder.

An instant of eerie shock, sparks and high voltage in Shamrock's mind. This is no rock, she thought, it's a ship! Sunk to the bottom . . .

She unfastened the reel from her belt, tied the line to the lowest rung of the ladder. Time jerked into high gear, the detective juggling possibilities so swiftly that she barely followed:

something someone invited her, connect riddle connect Ferrune connect *petal flowers,* connect psychometry, connect Stilton Ferret connect Avedoi Merek ?! connect Burrows connect Loch Stoat—time—connect palace ?! connect Nutmeg & Bergamont connect aqua-bees ?! *what is the pollen for?* connect Budgeron Ferret connect why ship, why sunk, when sunk—*time!*—how sunk, where built, connect Courtesies ?! connect Ferret Way ?! connect war connect *Paws of Knowledge, Volume 13* connect Dad and Mum connect bubbles? connect Curious Patterns ?! connect Miss Ginger connect your very own star . . . years tucked inside seconds as the detective watched the blur. —TIME—

TIME!

Shamrock touched her watch, unbelieving. In what had seemed no longer than a breath to her, the dive-limit marker had jumped beyond its redline. Too late, nearly, she must be on her way upward, she must decompress from the deep in stages, and without air to breathe, without time, she couldn't do it. Every second she stayed at this depth made it worse, made it less probable that she would survive unless she started upward minutes ago.

What is this ship?

She grasped the ladder in her paws, lifted herself from lakebed toward the quicksilver reflections, betting her life there would be a chamber above, an entrance to the ship.

Breaking the surface inside the chamber, Shamrock glistened like a sea otter on the rungs of the ladder, her light casting harsh shadows in this place that had been so long black. As her paws touched the ring-shaped floor of the air lock, she heard a distant click and the chamber was flooded in soft light.

All painted metal, the walls and ceiling were continuous curves, a simple place, unfurnished save for pawrails leading to the ladder and to the circle of water through which she had entered. To her left, an oval hatch, taller than Shamrock, closed.

At last we meet, she thought. Whoever had sent the message, the riddle in Ferrune, must wait not far away.

"Hallo?" she called.

There was no answer. No one came to meet her, nor had sign or notice been left for her. She shed her diving harness, fins and weight belt, set them by the floodlight at the ladder.

The locking wheel of the hatch was spun tight. Never had she seen a locked door, but seafarers needed them, she knew, for watertight security in the bulkheads of their ships.

She touched the metal wall. Impressions flickered behind her eyes, these plates under construction. Visions of a shipyard, larger than any she knew, thousands of ferrets at work on scaffolds, hoisting tools she had never seen, joining one curving piece to another.

Now a muffled metal clank echoed in the chamber, solid metal rose to seal the watery entrance. Shamrock heard the sound of air escaping, she felt the pressure change in her ears.

It won't be long. She stood quietly, assessing nearly to overload.

Why the silence? Somewhere someone must have turned the chamber lights on, they must have operated the air lock. Yet why would there be an air lock in a sunken ship? Why should there be air at all?

She relaxed, smiled at herself. There is a reason, she thought. There is always a reason, and before long each step of my mystery will make perfect sense.

Shortly she heard the whine of gears meshed, noticed the hatch locking wheel turn by itself, motor-driven, a hiss of air as it lifted from its seal and slid aside.

This is not a shipwreck, it is a working vessel underwater. A submarine! She shrugged aside a wave of questions. Whatever is supposed to happen, she thought, is happening.

She stepped through the hatchway, followed the turn of the passage once to the left then to the right, where it became a long straightaway, an access corridor down the center of the ship. The vessel, whatever it was, was not wrecked. Behind her, the hatch closed and locked by itself. Air hissed and echoed, gears hummed as the inner door sealed itself and the outer one opened again to the deeps.

Stenciled in Ferrune at the intersection of every corridor and passageway was a reference: ◀𝕩 –

↑⊗⊗, then: ◀⊗ – ↑⊗◇. P9 – C11, she translated, P9 – C10 . . . Every fifth hatch added a placard: λ。 ʀ⌒ ⊦⟩×ѕ`.

S for *submersible,* she thought, or *submarine.* The submarine *Rainbow.*

"Hallo?" There was no reply.

She followed passageway 9, faced on the starboard side with white steel entry hatches. Crew's quarters, she guessed.

Nearly to the end of the passage, she froze. Over the hatchway at C2 was mounted a crest, an emblem. Smaller than she remembered, but there was no mistaking.

Fastened to the steel was the image of a two-headed serpent: arrows in one claw, thunderbolts in the other, a fierce wicked thing, the color of emerald and coal, graven upon an oval of white.

She swallowed. How could an image . . . From . . . Has someone, she thought, somehow, read my mind . . . ?

Beneath confusion she noticed and questioned as always, observing, missing no detail, leaving reaction and emotion for a different time. Over the serpent had been slashed in Ferrune, one word in red paint: ⟩ѕ↑⅄

Note, she translated. The word baffled her.

She climbed to the emblem, her paws trembling up the steel web of the passageway, examined the letters.

The word had been painted by paw. It wasn't an *e,* the last character, but an exclamation point. Over the fierce picture had been painted the word *Not!*

How had a submarine come to the bottom of Loch Stoat; how could it mount an emblem that only Shamrock of all the ferrets in the world had imagined; why the scarlet word to mock it; *where is the crew?*

Under the weight of those questions, she dropped to the deck, stood away and took an eye-picture of the emblem: gazed steadily, closed her eyes, opened them. The image caught in her memory, line and color, every detail.

"Hallo!"

But for echoes of her call, the ship remained silent.

Now's a time to practice patience, thought Shamrock. Oh, patience, my weakest virtue.

The detective, fur nearly dry, continued through the last hatch at the end of the passageway, found herself standing on what appeared to be an airline flight deck, lit with the same even glow that filled the rest of the vessel.

Roomier than a flight deck, in fact, bounded about with a dozen silent viewscreens, banks of instruments and switches and control handles, crew station seats complete with wide seat belts, none of them occupied.

The walls unpainted, translucent blue-silver steel. She caught her breath. The walls were ferretmetal, and blazoned upon them an insignia in gold: two stars, one large, one small, joined by a sweeping curved pathway. The pattern from the cornfields.

She moved closer, observing, absorbing, analyzing, as though Mum and Dad had led her here by the paw, removed her blindfold, stepped back.

What is this place, Shamrock, what is it for? How was it built? By whom? When? Where? How did it come to Loch Stoat? Why have you been invited here, who opened the doors? What is the emblem? *What does this vessel mean?*

"I'm here!" Her voice echoed against the metal, as much her beginning statement of fact as a voice to be heard by another.

The place was empty, silent. No dials glowed, not a needle flickered.

Her eyes widened. Placards, instrument markings, labels, all of them were engraved in Ferrune. Oval ports looked into black water. Fastened to the sill of one port, a small blue vase, a silken flower within to make it homelike, a humble Shooting Star. . . .

The painting!

"*S* doesn't mean submarine," she whispered, numb. "*S is for starship!*"

Shamrock sank to the edge of the forwardmost seat, ahead of a half-circle of semi-couches. Not knowing she made a sound, she spoke into silence.

"This is where they sat, my ancestors, in these seats, they touched these controls, they flew this machine across the stars! They were *here*!"

They had come, her ancient fathers and mothers and the kits who would be Shamrock's great-grandparents hundreds of times removed, they had come in this ship, light-years from Ferra to Earth.

Her eyes filling with tears, the detective collapsed forward upon the control pedestal, face buried in her paws. Pressed against the metal of the console, her tears on the ancient instruments, she watched the landing in her mind, yearning toward her great-grandparents in wild discovering joy that felt like endless sorrow.

Visions unprompted.

There had been no Loch Stoat, then. When the first ferrets landed, this place was a level valley meadow. Softly had the ship touched the grass here as it had touched in fields to the south, gently had it settled to its final landing, magnetic engines at last gone quiet.

Behind her eyes she saw the ancients when they were young, when they were kits, brave and frightened at once, filled with resolve to make a home of this new place, a civilization built upon the Courtesies.

She felt their determination. They wouldn't write old history, they'd live it new. Why condemn the future, recording wars that didn't deserve to be honored in memory, why pass word through time, immortalizing names that stood for hatred and battle?

They who mocked that fierce serpent had vowed to honor only the highest their culture had been in spite of it, they vowed to surpass that highest, themselves. The colonists had survived every hazard the universe could lay before them, for the sake of their kits and a new beginning.

Now Shamrock Ferret, one of those unborn who had called her parents to the stars, lay sobbing in love for ancestors long dead, alive again in her heart.

CHAPTER 23

"Would you care for tea, Miss Shamrock?"

Burrows Ferret stood before the flight deck console, water-drops glistening still in his fur. Behind him, another animal, unrecognized through the detective's tears.

"Burrows!" As much a sob as a cry of delight.

"Yes, ma'am." He looked about the room. "You found it!"

"They came . . . all of them, they came from Ferra! *Burrows, this is their ship!*"

"It is."

"You knew?"

"No. We followed you down. We know now."

"The legend's true. We came from the stars!"

"You have a great deal of evidence, Miss Shamrock." He turned to the other animal, nodded, turned back.

"Burrows . . ." Shamrock rose and hugged her partner, buried her face in the soft fur of his chest, tears on sable. He stood quietly, sheltering her.

At last Burrows made his introduction: "Miss Shamrock, I'm pleased to present Miss Nutmeg Ferret, of Nutmeg—"

Shamrock gasped, whirled to the animal she had admired for so long. The charcoal dust had washed from the captain's fur in the long dive from the boat. Now, still wet, it shone that soft spice-color, the eyes unchanged, noticing all.

Smiling at the young detective's startlement, Nutmeg completed the introduction with a wave to Shamrock's partner: ". . . and Bergamont."

Shamrock turned, felt her knees weaken. "Mr. Burrows? *You're* Bergamont Ferret?"

"The late Bergamont Ferret," said her partner. "The erstwhile Bergamont. I stumble sometimes, when cameras come round."

"You charmed us from the beginning, Shamrock," said Nutmeg, "since before the beginning. The Case of the Invisible Clock, remarkable—twin ferrets, we discover—well done! And the Case of the Curious Patterns. We were puzzled, everyone was, and when you found the artists, and the mouse explained . . ." Nutmeg nodded to the emblem on the wall. "How did you know the patterns were from *Rainbow,* before you found the ship?"

"I didn't." Shamrock smiled at her heroine. "But give me a day here, ma'am, and I'll tell you all about it." Her mind raced. So much to say! "Miss Nutmeg, the aqua-bees! Did you notice? Their hive is aboard this ship. Do you suppose that means . . ."

". . . they're not bees at all?" asked Nutmeg.

Shamrock's observer within stood back, happy: here she is, the kit who once hauled encyclopedias home from the library, standing now, sharing ideas and matching wits with the celebrated Nutmeg & Bergamont.

The stuff of family, it thought. With the adventures we choose and the mysteries we solve we build our own credentials, write our own introduction to others around the world who value adventure and mystery themselves.

Shamrock Ferret, become a celebrity? Bright as she is, thought the observer within, she'll enjoy it.

CHAPTER 24

Once every century, the atomic clock strikes *Open and Search*.
Once every century the external access door slides open near *Rainbow*'s dorsal thruster.
Once every century I am launched.

Arcs and radials, I hum. Thousand-paw radius, ten-thousand-paw, one megapaw, ten megapaws, a hundred.

NSSD: No Suitable Storage Device.
Return to ship.
Monitor Hive Environment Nominal, Data-Bees
  in Rest.
Reset clock.
Shut down.

Once every century, I search.
I have searched 106 times.
After the thirty-ninth century, the atmosphere
  changed from free nitrogen and oxygen to ice
  and then to water, the ship at the bottom of a
  deepening lake of this substance.

Recording, Cycle 107:

Instruction—*Open and Search*.
External Access Door—*Clear*.
Door—*Open*.
Data-Bee—*Launch*.

I hum through water.

I begin search, thousand-paw radius.
NSSD.

I hum through air.

I begin search, ten-thousand-paw radius.
SDL: Storage Device Located. Range: 2,127 paws.
  Azimuth: 283 degrees.

I return to ship.

I activate Data-Bee Hive Wake-Up sequence.

I lock door open.

I reset my mission identity from Search Bee to Transfer Bee.

I begin Ferret Information Transfer, Energy Conservation Protocol, Low Volume Transmission.

I access ship's data center.

I download first kilopack, Section One Outline:

1. To Our Grandkits
2. Who We Are
3. History of Ferra
4. Why We Came to Earth
5. Reenergizing *Rainbow*
6. Starship Operation
7. Navigation, and the Way Home
8. Ship's Logs and Records
9. Technical Data

I return to door.

I launch.

I hum direct to palace, thence through air shafts to archive storage below main library.

I confirm upload will not interfere with ferret computer operating system.

I upload first kilopack Section One Outline into unused disc space.

I return to ship.

I access ship's data center.

I download next kilopack Section One in sequence.

I continue transfer in one-kilopack units with other
   data-bees to upload twenty thousand gigapacks
   or until alternate instructions from ferrets.
I override following century cycles as required until
   upload complete.

I like my job.

⌢

Wings buzzing cobalt silver in the sunlight, dusky
pearl under the moon, aqua-bees emerge in tiny
splashes from Loch Stoat, trailing misty spray from
their wings, on course for the palace in Mustelania.
They are small, fly swiftly and are rarely seen, even
at close range.

CHAPTER 25

Darkness might have fallen on the loch above; within *Rainbow,* the light was cool and even, the three ferrets at the navigator's station, star charts for a desktop.

"You know the feeling, Miss Nutmeg," said Shamrock, warm and at home now with the one who had been her heroine. "When I looked over the hatch in the passageway, and there was the serpent . . ." She shrugged with delight.

"Proof?" asked the other, that quiet voice.

"Proof! Otherwise, my psychometry, it could have been a dream, my vision just a theory. No one would have believed it was a choice we made. He was an example, Avedoi Merek. One ferret, one personal decision, on his own: *I withdraw my consent from evil . . .*"

"The rest of them listened," said Nutmeg, "knowing he was right. And they withdrew their consent, as well. Was that it?"

"To this day! All of us do it, still. Not one deed, but millions: every animal, every choice, every day. All of us, a continuous, undying golden deed."

The celebrity smiled at her young colleague. "A solution so beautiful is probably true," she said. "But tell me—you can prove that it began with Avedoi Merek?"

The way Nutmeg asked, thought Shamrock . . . something was wrong.

She laser-flashed over her case. All was in order: the sign of a war-serpent that she could not know existed but for her vision: Avedoi Merek standing alone, choosing his highest right. Her discovery of that very emblem over the passageway in this sunken starship. Evidence.

It was the snake that proved the vision to me, thought Shamrock, and in that instant she caught the flaw that Nutmeg hinted: the difference between subjective and objective, between deduced and tangible.

Shamrock laughed, mortified, lifted her paws to cover her eyes. "Oh, bless my whiskers," she said, her voice muffled in the quiet. "The snake proved the case *to me*!"

The sign, the arrows and thunderbolts were concrete, evidence to examine in the passageway above the hatch at C2. But Shamrock's story, though true, was no proof that any golden deed had ever occurred.

Other ferrets would believe her, for ferrets honor the truth that each perceives, but other ferrets hadn't been in the council hall with her, hadn't vaulted across time to the fires of an ancient war, hadn't watched civilization turn on the point of Avedoi Merek's example, the declaration of his highest right. All of this had been Shamrock Ferret's perception, it belonged to no other animal alive.

At last she folded her paws in her lap, her smile a little sad. She knew what had happened, and she would be alone in her knowing for so long as she lived.

"We can win them all, Miss Shamrock," said Burrows, "but we don't do it very often."

Nutmeg rose. "Have you considered," she said softly, "that you may have solved a case, a different one, which has never been opened?"

Shamrock shook her head.

Nutmeg caught Burrows' eye, and he nodded, go ahead.

"Let's call it the Case of the Missing Magnet. Have you ever wondered, Miss Shamrock, why ferrets love celebrities? You have. You know we love them because we're curious, and we're a civilization of models for each other. What other culture but ours calls on celebrity to show its highest morality?"

"None," said Shamrock. "But the Courtesies are in our hearts, ma'am, they're the first morals we learn."

"The Courtesies are ideas," said Nutmeg. "Each of us, we live our own example of kindness and respect, of excellence in whatever we do, of how to think and speak and act in any situation. But celebrities are our examples. They start with nothing but a dream, most of them, they find the courage to follow what they know is right, no matter what. If I've been an example for you, Miss Shamrock, today you're an example for me."

"You're an example for everyone, Nutmeg! *'Now why would this be?'* When anyone finds a mystery, they start with your words, they—"

Burrows cut her off, not harsh but firm. "She's asking you to be an example, too, Miss Shamrock. She's asking you to join her. Onstage, in front of the world."

The interruption was an act so astonishing that his partner was left midsentence, her mouth open, staring at him.

"If you would let go your humility," Burrows continued, "this would be no surprise. You are a brilliant detective, insightful, original, entertaining, unafraid. You cannot light such a firework of mind without expecting others to notice, and notice we have. We've been watching since you were a kit, and now it's time for others to watch, too."

"You've been watching . . . ?"

"We gave you tests, some cases we didn't solve," said Nutmeg. "But with us or without, you're on your way, Shamrock, and before long you'll be known around the world. It's not easy, all day every day, standing for the best in everyone. But there is a network. We can help."

"You're kind to believe in me, Miss Nutmeg, but I don't want to be a celebrity."

"Why not?" The words a little sad. Can she pass every test but this?

"The attention, the glare, the photos, newsferrets asking what you think, and why, always why . . ."

If soft words could shout, Nutmeg Ferret's did that moment. "Always-why is the way you grew up! Always-why is the love that drives you on! And beyond always-why is always-how. Kits around the world will pin your picture to their bedroom wall: 'How would Shamrock solve my case? How would Shamrock think if she were here? What would Shamrock do if she were me?'

"They won't know they're building their morality on your example, yours and other celebrities', but that's what they'll do. Your highest right will become theirs, Shamrock Ferret. If you slip, so will they!"

"Or you can retire," said Burrows, with a little smile. "There we can't help you much."

"What if I fail," she said, "what if I miss my highest right, what if I let them down?"

"Thought experiment, Miss Shamrock," said Nutmeg. "Can you imagine yourself setting out to become the highest, the most brilliant animal you know how to be, and *failing*?"

☁

For the next hour, Shamrock wandered alone through the passageways of the starship, considering her highest right. She had been offered a chance to touch the lives of millions of kits. Accept, and she must give up her personal privacy for the rest of her life. Accept, and never again could she appear in public, no matter how courteous that public might be, without someone knowing who she was, connecting her with an ideal of mind and spirit, expecting her to shine that forth at all times in all places.

In her psychometry she held an object in her paws, sifting out with her spirit to find what it could tell of its past. Now the object held her, the starship *Rainbow* surrounding her with its ferretmetal memories, crew and colonists long dead, all of them seeking a world that would never again lift up the thoughtless to lead the unknowing into war.

Examples.

A vision passed through her heart: long ago, some ferrets had forgotten that others beside themselves love their mates and their kits, that others beside themselves cherish freedom to fashion all manner of invention and business and comedy and art.

bestseller list, just below Danielle Ferret's *Veronique's Kit*.

Both books moved down a place in the next issue as Avedoi Merek's *The Ferret Way* hit the top of the list—a first, said the tabloids, for an author over a hundred centuries old.

How easy, forgetting, for Us and Them to arise, one fearing the other, one defending from the other.

Another vision washed over her: aftermath. Mates and kits now dead and dying, all at once the scorched survivors understood each other. As he spoke those few words to Ferra, common sense found in Avedoi Merek a spirit who with one breath, one personal decision, cast off evil.

When all that we love lies in ruins, how simple it is to vow from the deepest well of our soul:

Whatever harm I would do to another, I shall do first to myself.

So do all of us, promise. Every elder, every peer, every kit:

Before I harm you, I shall harm myself.

Before you harm me, you will harm yourself.

Therefore, as I refuse to harm myself, you shall live unharmed as well, you and your mates and your kits and your homes and your cities.

Therefore, as you refuse to harm yourself, I shall live unharmed as well, me and my mate and my kits and my homes and my cities.

Upon this promise stands unshatterable, adventurous peace.

So strong the hum of her vision that the detective swayed, reached for support to the steel of the hatch at P4 – C91.

Avedoi Merek had walked through fire, he and all the animals who had survived the war on Ferra, and the power of their drive, rejecting evil, had flung *Rainbow* across the stars.

The echoes of their promise swept across their great-grandkit, lifted her above fears for her future.

I shall make each choice and live each day to my highest sense of right.

Shamrock Ferret let go the steel. Kits need all the examples they can find. As Nutmeg stood for me, so let me stand, please, for one other kit.

She nodded, decision done. So shall it be. Goodbye, privacy.

☁

Hours after her decision, through Stilton Ferret's MusTelCo media as well as by enthusiastic competitors around the world, a civilization learned that the legends of Ferra hadn't been fables at all.

Detective Lands Spaceship at Palace! cried the headlines, Burrows to work at once with the correction: Shamrock Ferret did not fly the starship nor did she land it, she merely discovered a craft that may have brought the first colonists, and the Courtesies, to Earth.

FerreTV ran its version of the correction: *Modest Sleuth Discovers Starship, Proves* Ferret Way—*Story at 11:00.*

"The first rule of celebrity," Burrows told her: "There will be distortion."

Shamrock hosted a two-disc videotour of the *Rainbow,* the program running day and night for viewers hypnotized by its scenes on cable and network television and across the ferretnet, with links for kits to sites on astronomy, physics, metallurgy, particle mechanics, psychology, aviation, space technology, archaeology, history, mythology, underwater exploration, psychic science and advertising.

She could not prove that one golden deed had changed the world forever, switched its polarity from negative to positive. In time, she didn't care. It is not what we prove to others, that matters to the heart, but what we know within.

Her book, *Imagining Fact: Avedoi Merek in the Council of Ferra,* appeared on the *Mustelid Weekly*

CHAPTER 26

Far down a street of ferret houses, nearly to the end, stood the home of Oliver Ferret, still a kit but smart as any creature alive, his neighbors thought, when it came to puzzles.

He loved riddles and mysteries, his mind a sponge for patterns. He discovered, watching the empty static of an unused television channel, that by willing it so, he could make whirling cyclones of black and white appear on the screen, turn them clockwise, now counterclockwise, shift them into squares, into letters of the alphabet, into words that came from within.

The kit had intuitions for the way nature works, why clouds tumble as they do, and rivers and winds about hills and mountains. Now was he beginning to dream the way stars work, and atoms, and where the atoms begin and why.

☁

"That's it, yes!" said the photographer for *Behind the Mask,* his face hidden in camera and telephoto lens, photoflash popping softly from the reflector on its stand. "Very nice. The star map a little closer, please, Miss Shamrock? Yes. Perfect. Very nice. Thank you. Forget the camera now, just go ahead and finish up with Jillibar. I'll get a couple of pickup shots while you talk, if that's all right?"

"Certainly," said Shamrock.

The writer had been waiting, patient to finish her interview. *Behind the Mask* wasn't a photo magazine, but this would be a big spread and photos were important. Some scenes though, she thought, photos can't show. She touched the button of her recorder.

"A lot of our readers are young," said Jillibar Ferret. "If you could give one idea to kits, Miss Shamrock

. . . if you could say one word to yourself when you were a kit, what would you say?"

One word, thought Shamrock, one idea. "Trust," she said. "There's a light, when we close our eyes, the light of what we want to do more than anything else in all the world. Trust that light. Follow, wherever it leads."

The writer listened to silence after the sentence, touched the recorder off.

"That's it. Thank you so much, Miss Shamrock. We appreciate your time this afternoon. May I call when the story's done, check that I've got it right?"

"Whenever you wish," said the detective. She smiled at the writer. "There's a lot to say, isn't there?"

Jillibar Ferret nodded. "Somehow, I think you'll get your chance to say everything you want to say."

Her visitors gone, Shamrock slipped downstairs from her midtown office, a hidden passage to the alleyway entrance.

"Don't forget to turn it on before you knock on the door," she said, adjusting the flower-camera in Burrows' scarf. "I need to watch, but he'll notice everything, and if you're fussing with this . . ."

"Don't you worry," said her partner, rubbing chalk to lighten his mask, brushing his fur backward here and there. "I did it for you, didn't I?"

"M-hm." She nodded. "And I knew something was up."

She took the brush as he finished, set it on a shelf. "Do not call Oliver by name; you do not know his name, remember. And you're going to stop next door, this time. He's going to ask the neighbors . . ."

"Of course," said Burrows. "I forgot, with you. But you managed to turn out all right, Miss Shamrock. You passed your tests, though you may have suspected . . ." He nodded briskly to the detective, stepped out the door to his *Paws of Knowledge* van, every bit the salesferret.

Shamrock Ferret laughed. "Oh, Mr. Burrows," she called, shaking her head, "you might want to take this along."

He gritted his teeth in alarm, returned for his sample volume, a book by now a little tattered:

Paws of Knowledge, Volume 13: Megalith to Nudibranch.